Alligator Tails and Crocodile Cakes

NICOLA MOON

ILLUSTRATED BY
ANDY ELLIS

KINGFISHER

BOSTON

For my parents—N. M.
To Hayley—A. E.

KINGFISHER
a Houghton Mifflin Company imprint
222 Berkeley Street
Boston, Massachusetts 02116
www.houghtonmifflinbooks.com

First published by Kingfisher in 1996
This edition published in 2005
2 4 6 8 10 9 7 5 3 1
1TR/0305/AJT/PW(SACH)/115MA/F

LIBRARY OF CONGRESS CATALOGING-IN-PUBLICATION DATA
Moon, Nicola.
Alligator tails and crocodile cakes/Nicola Moon; illustrated by
Andy Ellis.—1st American ed.
p. cm. — (I am reading)
Summary: High-spirited Alligator and his patient friend Crocodile
play hide-and-seek and bake a cake.
[1. Alligators—Fiction. 2. Crocodiles—Ficiton. 3. Hide-and
-seek—Fiction. 4. Baking—Fiction. 5. Cleanliness—Fiction.
6. Friendship—Fiction] I. Ellis, Andy, ill. II. Title.
III. Series
PZ7.M776A1 1997
[E]—dc20 96-28974 CIP AC

ISBN 0-7534-5853-5
ISBN 978-07534-5853-2

Printed in India

Contents

Hide-and-Seek

Crocodile was playing hide-and-seek

with his friend Alligator.

Crocodile closed his eyes

and started counting.

"One, two, three, four, five, six . . ."

Alligator looked for somewhere to hide.

He found a big tree.

He stood behind the tree

and made himself as

as tall as he could.

"Ready or not, here I come," called
Crocodile. He looked to the left.

He looked to the right.

He looked up, and he looked down.

And then . . .

"I found you! I found you!

I can see your tail!" he sang.

7

"I want to hide again," said Alligator.

"And this time you won't find me."

So Crocodile closed his eyes

and started counting.

"One, two, three, four, five, six, seven . . ."

Alligator looked for somewhere to hide.

He found a space between two rocks.

He squeezed himself in

and made himself as thin as he could.

9

"Ready or not, here I come!" called

Crocodile. He looked to the left.

He looked to the right.

He looked up, and he looked down.

And then . . .

"I found you! I found you!

I can see your tail!" he sang.

"I want to hide again," said Alligator.

"And this time you really won't find me."

So Crocodile closed his eyes

and started counting.

"One, two, three, four,

five, six, seven, eight . . ."

Alligator looked for somewhere to hide.

He found a hedge.

He wriggled under the hedge
and made himself as flat as he could.

"Ready or not, here I come!" called

Crocodile. He looked to the left.

He looked to the right.

He looked up, and he looked down.

And then . . .

"I found you! I found you!

I can see your tail!" he sang.

"I want to hide again," said Alligator.

"And this time you really, definitely

won't find me."

So Crocodile closed his eyes

and started counting.

"One, two, three, four,

five, six, seven, eight, nine . . ."

Alligator looked for somewhere to hide.

He found an old barrel.

He climbed in and curled up.

He made himself as small as he could.

"Ready or not, here I come!" called
Crocodile. He looked to the left.
He looked to the right.
He looked up, and he looked down.
And then . . .

"I found you! I found you!
I can see your tail!" he sang.

"I want to hide again," said Alligator.
"And this time you really, definitely,
positively won't be able to find me.
NO WAY!"
So Crocodile closed his eyes
and started counting.

"One, two, three, four,
five, six, seven, eight, nine, ten . . ."

This time Alligator didn't look
for somewhere to hide.
He crept up close behind Crocodile
and stayed as still and quiet as he could.

"Ready or not, here I come!" called Crocodile. He looked to the left.

He looked to the right.

He looked up,

and he looked down.

But he didn't look behind him.

"BOO!" shouted Alligator.

"I knew you wouldn't find me!"

"My turn to hide now," said Crocodile.
"Make sure that you don't leave your
tail sticking out," said Alligator.

Crocodile and Alligator
Bake a Cake

Crocodile and Alligator were baking a cake.
Crocodile had his grandma's cookbook
and an enormous mixing bowl.

Alligator was opening all the cupboards.

"We need some flour," said Crocodile.

"What's flour?" said Alligator.

"It's white and soft and dusty,"
said Crocodile.

"And it's in a blue bag."
As he spoke, a blue bag
wobbled
and toppled
and landed POOF!
on the floor near
Alligator's feet.

"Like this?" asked Alligator.

"Yes," said Crocodile. "That's flour."

Crocodile put four big spoonfuls

of flour into the bowl.

Alligator swept up the mess.

"We need some eggs," said Crocodile.

"How many?" asked Alligator.

"Two," said Crocodile. "Two large eggs."

Alligator picked out two big, brown eggs

from the carton.

"I saw someone juggle eggs once,"

he said. "Like this . . ."

SPLAT! SPLOSH!

Alligator wasn't very good at juggling.

Luckily there were two more eggs left.

Crocodile cracked the eggs

against the side of the bowl,

opened the shells,

and let the eggs

drop onto

the flour.

"You have to be careful, Alligator."

"I will," said Alligator,

cleaning up the mess.

"We need some butter," said Crocodile.

"Where will I find that?" asked Alligator.

"In the fridge," said Crocodile.

"In a large white tub."

Alligator opened the fridge

and took out the large white tub.

He tried to open the lid.

It was very tight.

"Can you open it for me, please?"

Crocodile pulled
and tugged
and heaved
and . . . PLOP!

The lid flew off,
and Crocodile
dropped the tub
on the floor.
Upside down.

31

"You have to be more careful, Crocodile,"
laughed Alligator.

"Very funny," said Crocodile,
and he picked up the tub.
Luckily there was still some butter left.
Alligator wiped up the mess.

"We need some sugar," said Crocodile.

"I know where the sugar is," said Alligator.

"I like sugar."

He reached up and carefully lifted down

the container marked SUGAR.

"Be careful that you don't slip . . ."

said Crocodile.

CRASH!

It was too late.

Alligator sat on the floor

looking miserable,

covered in sticky sugar.

"I don't think I'm very good

at making cakes," he said.

"You just need to be more careful,"

said Crocodile.

He measured

what was left of the sugar.

Alligator looked sadly at the mess.

"All we need now are some raisins,"
said Crocodile.

"You can measure them if you want,"
he added.

Alligator cheered up.

He measured the raisins
and put them into a little dish.

"We'll add them later," explained Crocodile.

"May I taste one?" asked Alligator.

"Just one," said Crocodile,

who was busy plugging in the mixer.

Alligator ate a raisin.

Then another one.

And another . . .

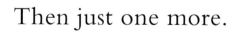

Then just one more.

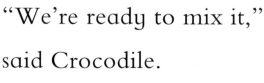

"We're ready to mix it,"
said Crocodile.
"Stand back!"

Crocodile turned on the mixer.

WHOOSH!

The flour and eggs

and butter and sugar

spun around in the bowl so fast

that it made Alligator dizzy.

"Is that really going to turn into a cake?"

asked Alligator,

looking at the creamy mixture.

"A delicious cake," said Crocodile.

He turned off the mixer.

"Now it's time for you

to stir in the raisins."

Crocodile poured
the mixture into
a big, round pan

and put it into the oven to bake.
"Now we can clean up the mess," he said.
"And when we're finished,
the cake will be ready."

They mopped

and swept

and wiped

and polished the floor.

Crocodile washed

the mixing bowl and the spoon

and cleaned the mixer.

"Mmmm!" said Alligator.

"I smell something good."

"I think the cake is ready,"

said Crocodile.

He lifted it out of the oven very carefully.

When the cake was cool,

Crocodile cut two huge slices

and poured two glasses of lemonade.

"Scrumptious!" said Alligator.

"I'm good at *eating* cakes!"

"There don't seem to be many raisins in it,"

said Crocodile.

"May I have another piece?"

asked Alligator.

"Only if you sweep up the crumbs,"

said Crocodile.

"Just look at the mess you're making!"

About the author and illustrator

Nicola Moon was a teacher before she began writing books for children. Nicola says, "When I was a child, hide-and-seek was one of my favorite games. I can remember helping make cakes, too, just like Alligator."

Andy Ellis has written and illustrated many children's books. He also works on cartoons for television. "Trying to make an alligator and a crocodile look friendly wasn't easy, but I hope the readers will think I've succeeded!"

Strategies for Independent Readers

Predict
Think about the cover, illustrations, and the title of the book. What do you think this book will be about? While you are reading think about what may happen next and why.

Monitor
As you read ask yourself if what you're reading makes sense. If it doesn't, reread, look at the illustrations, or read ahead.

Question
Ask yourself questions about important ideas in the story such as what the characters might do or what you might learn.

Phonics
If there is a word that you do not know, look carefully at the letters, sounds, and word parts that you do know. Blend the sounds to read the word. Ask yourself if this is a word you know. Does it make sense in the sentence?

Summarize
Think about the characters, the setting where the story takes place, and the problem the characters faced in the story. Tell the important ideas in the beginning, middle, and end of the story.

Evaluate
Ask yourself questions like: Did you like the story? Why or why not? How did the author make the story come alive? How did the author make the story fun to read? How well did you understand the story? Maybe you can understand it better if you read it again!